chef Dough Dough

3-31-12

TO: Eliza + Louise
Eat Well, Be Strong, Live Long
Chef Dough Dough

Bill Hurtt-el

To my brood of Grandchildren to come,
My kitchen is waiting.

To all the Grisanti kids who laughed every time they heard me read a Chef Dough Dough story.

Hallie, you helped me realize that the length of a child's attention span is shorter than the length of my imagination.

To my closest friends who read copy after copy and helped me make change after change.

Wendy and Anita, my biggest cheerleaders, you believed and encouraged me because you saw the BIG picture.

Heather, you are the most diligent and punctual project manager: you picked up the ball and ran with it.

Paula, your gift of encouragement has been a blessing on the road to bringing Chef Dough Dough back to life. God's will for me has been made clear through your constant prayer and mentoring.

To my four children: George, Gavrion, Tasia and Margo, thank you for letting me go on to mother another generation of children.

To my husband Peter, your love for me and my endeavors is the reason we have a book. My morning coffee lovingly brought to my bedside is the jolt that gets me going everyday. Se Agapo!

Requests for permission to make copies of any part of the work should be submitted online at www.chefdoughdough.com

ISBN 978-0-615-51689-9

Chef Dough Dough
&
the GIANT
Purple Grapes

Written by Dodo Grisanti Katsotis
Illustrated by Bill Huettel

Finally summer had arrived. Days of playing, swimming and eating would last forever. Joey slept late his first day off from school. A cinnamon roll, a stack of pancakes, two eggs and a bowl of Flutter Mutter Flakes all served up on his camping plates in the tree house was his first summer night's dream.

To his delight, the smell of his dad cooking in the kitchen
woke him. His dad was the best breakfast chef ever. Joey
loved sitting in the kitchen watching him flip eggs in the pan.

Just as Joey took the last bite of his pancake, his best bud Josh burst through the door and said, "Hey doodle head, quit shoveling all that food in your mouth. Let's go play in the tree house!"

"I'll race you there," teased Josh. "On your mark, get set, go!" they shouted.

Under the tree they whispered the code, "Oopa, Loopa, Dooda, Da," and sealed it with their 12-pat handshake.

Josh tugged on
the rope and quickly
shimmied up. Joey
ambled up at a
tortoise's pace.

"Let's play Nugga Tugga," said Joey. For hours, the boys played their favorite game.

GRRRRHHHH!

"What was that?" Josh said with a fright.

"Don't be such a scaredy cat," said Joey. "That was my stomach growling. Let's go inside and get some donuts."

"Whoo whoo wants shuga shuga sugar?" said a voice from the window.

Just then the boys looked up to see an old blue and silver owl that had landed on the tree house window sill.

"Who are you?" they asked.

"I'm Oscar Owl, pleased to meet you. I'm from the Land of the Purple Moon and I'm here to help my old friend, Chef Dough Dough.

"Whoo Whoo Whoo..." called Owl.

Instantly the tree house began to shake.

"Donuts? Donuts? I dare you to try some grapes!" Chef Dough Dough shrilly shouted as she squeezed through a hidden hatch.

With a wave of her hand over her hat she commanded, "Stir to the left, stir to the right, into my sight, a yummy delight."

Giant purple grapes popped out and
filled the tree house floor.

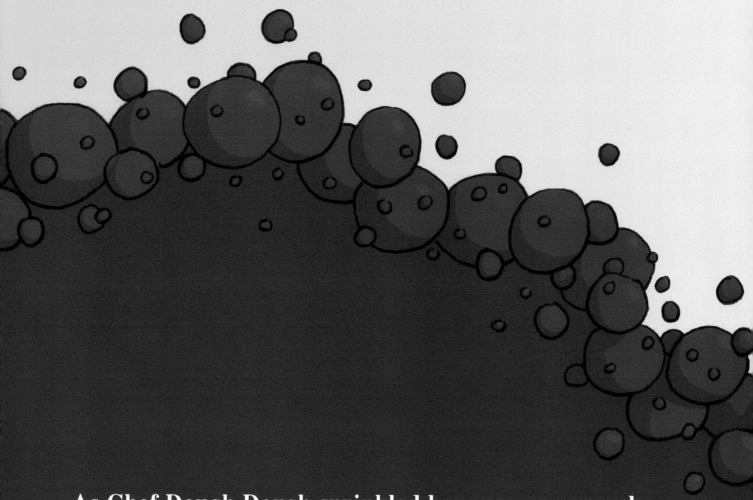

As Chef Dough Dough sprinkled bananarama crumbs over the grapes, Joey's mouth began to water.

"Go ahead and try one," Chef Dough Dough insisted.

"Ok, I'll do it!" said Joey.

He snatched up a giant grape and an explosion of flavor filled his mouth. As he chewed, purple juice dripped down his chin and a smile of delight spread from ear to ear.

Josh watched and reluctantly popped one in his mouth as well.

"Wow," Josh said with a mouthful, "these are awesome!"

The boys began tossing the grapes
in the air and then at each other.

Joey's dad came running out of the house.

"Boys what's all that noise? It's time to come in for a snack," he shouted.

   As the boys walked into the kitchen, they were amazed at
what they saw. On the counter was a huge silver platter with
a donut tower that touched the ceiling. It was filled with
rainbow donuts, chocolate moose track donuts, cinnamon
swirl donuts, cherry, strawberry and ice cream filled donuts.

   "Voila, a tasty treat for my backyard warriors," said
Joey's dad.

Joey and Josh looked at each other, both feeling so satisfied. They smiled and Joey said, "No thanks, Dad. We just ate a bunch of GIANT PURPLE GRAPES!"

Joey pulled some smooshed grapes out of his pocket and offered them to his dad. "Dad, have some! We dare you to!"

Joey's dad cringed at the sight of the crushed grapes.

At that moment, the three were startled when Chef Dough Dough popped out of the pantry. In the pocket of her apron was a baby grape vine.

"Let's go plant this vine and you can grow fresh grapes to eat all summer long," she urged.

"I can dig that," said Joey's Dad.

The boys grabbed their buckets and shovels and
ran to the yard to dig a hole.

About the Author...

Dolores Grisanti Katsotis' passion for food began at an early age. She is a third generation chef destined to make a career in the culinary arts after growing up in her family's Italian restaurants. "Dodo," as she is affectionately known to her family and friends, is a graduate of The Culinary Institute of America in Hyde Park, New York. That is where she launched her professional career that has taken her all over the country. She has worked as a chef in New Jersey, Hawaii, Maryland, California and her native state, Tennessee. She has also owned and operated several restaurants with her husband whom she met while attending culinary school. Her first cookbook was co-authored with her father and is titled *Wining and Dining with John Grisanti*.

While home schooling her four young children, she discovered her passion for educating children. She created an innovative curriculum focused on science and food that was offered as a summer camp at The Children's Museum of Memphis, and was featured in the August 1994 issue of Southern Living Magazine. This is where she coined her pen name, "Chef Dough Dough."

The following year Chef Dough Dough collaborated with the Make-A-Wish foundation and wrote her first children's book *Cooking Adventures with Chef Dough Dough*. 10,000 copies were printed and all proceeds benefited the granting of wishes to terminally ill children. In 1997, she was honored as Donor of the Decade by the Make a Wish Foundation. Her love of children has fueled her devotion to help kids through the Memphis Junior League, St Jude Children's Research Hospital and the Salvation Army.

Katsotis has been featured in The Commercial Appeal, The Memphis Flyer, Taste Magazine, Food Arts Magazine, Memphis Magazine, Frederick Magazine and At Home Tennessee. In one of her shining moments she was chosen as a finalist for an "AUGIE" award at The Culinary Institute of America, for the category of "Most Creative Use of Resources in Business and Industry, Health Care and Education."

Dodo resides in Collierville, Tennessee with her husband Peter. They have four children, George, Gavrion, Tasia, Margo and two dogs, Chad and Bella.

CPSIA information can be obtained
at www.ICGtesting.com
Printed in the USA
271458LV00002B